ONIONS
MEAN I LOVE YOU

D1604663

WRITTEN BY
GINA LEHMAN

ILLUSTRATED BY
MARIA GRANTIS

This book belongs to:

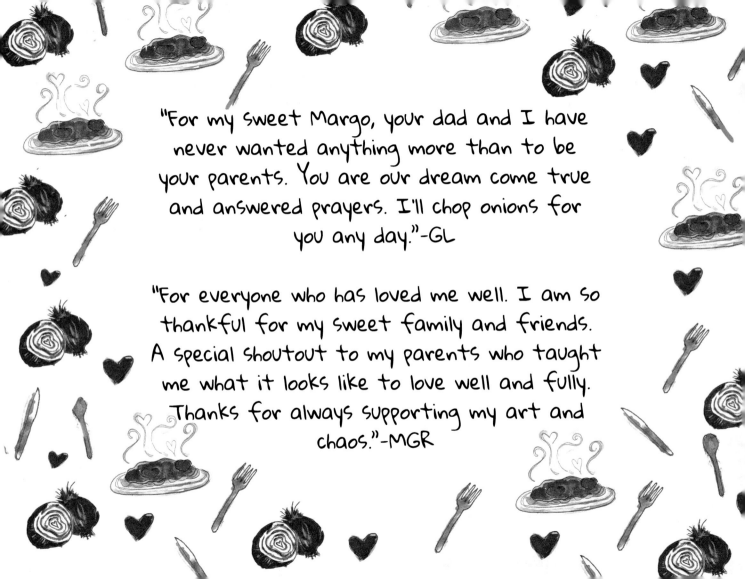

"For my sweet Margo, your dad and I have never wanted anything more than to be your parents. You are our dream come true and answered prayers. I'll chop onions for you any day."-GL

"For everyone who has loved me well. I am so thankful for my sweet family and friends. A special shoutout to my parents who taught me what it looks like to love well and fully. Thanks for always supporting my art and chaos."-MGR

Today is my birthday!

As a special treat my mom is making my favorite dinner, spaghetti and meatballs! Her special recipe, just for me!

My mom is chopping up an onion when suddenly, I see that she's crying! "Mommy!" I shout, "Why are you so sad?" I run over and hug her as tight as I can. She always hugs me when I'm sad.

She puts down the knife and laughs. "Oh, honey, I am not sad. Chopping onions always makes me cry!" I look up at her, feeling so confused. "Well, why do you chop onions if they make you cry?"

She kneels and puts her hands on my shoulders. "Because onions are a part of my special recipe that you love, and I love you!"

As we eat dinner, I think about what my mommy said and start thinking about all the ways you can show love.

My dog must really love me because he sleeps next to my feet every night to keep them warm. I would not want my face near anyone's feet, pee-yew!

The mail carrier must really, really love me because she always delivers our mail, even when there is rain or snow!

I know my school bus driver must love me because
he wakes up bright and early to make sure
everyone gets to school on time.

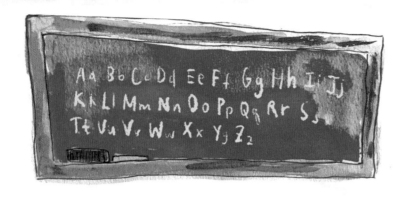

I know my teacher must really love me because he teaches me something new every day. He also helps to make sure I really understand!

Everyone shows me how much they love me,
and I want to show them too.

As I blow out the
candles on my cake,
I make a wish that
someday...

I will cook for my family, and
I will chop onions too.

SHOW LOVE hERE

Use these pages to draw people who show you they love you every day!

WRITTEN BY
GINA LEHMAN

Gina is a wife to her husband Brad, and a mother to her daughter Margo, and three dogs Betsey, Blondie, and Denny. The illustrations of the three-legged Chihuahua are inspired by Denny! She self-published this book while undergoing cancer treatment, a time when she truly felt how powerful even the smallest acts of kindness can be.

Thank you for reading!

ILLUSTRATED BY

MARIA G RANTIS

Maria is currently a student studying Graphic Design at UW-Madison. In addition to design, she loves creating art, especially illustration. She comes from a family of artists and people who always encouraged her creativity. Her family means everything to her.

Thank you for looking at my drawings! I hope you enjoyed!

THE END

Made in the USA
Middletown, DE
17 July 2022

69396697R00015